Dear Parents/Teachers:

Yay! Your child/student is interested in
The goal: reading on their own and lovi

Waldorf Readers are designed to help your child/student enjoy the learning process. Our Readers have 4 levels to guide your child/student to independent reading.

Each level collection has interesting stories, unique characters and colorful illustrations. All Waldorf Readers are original works with characters your child/student will enjoy. Waldorf Publishing strives to accommodate a full reading experience for any child/student at any reading level.

Waldorf Readers will entertain your child/student level by level.

Spark Reading   **Preschool-Kindergarten**
-Large font and easy words
-Illustrations to accompany the storyline
-No more than two syllables

Level 1 Waldorf Readers introduce children/students to reading. Sentences are short and simple. Using phonics skills, children/students will sound out words.

Read Together   **Preschool-Grade 1**
-Short sentences
-Easy to understand stories
-Simple vocabulary
-No more than two syllables

Level 2 Waldorf Readers keep the excitement for reading strong. Sentences will include bigger words and more in depth story lines, which are sure to entertain.

Independent Reading   **Grade 1-3**
-Exciting and relatable characters
-Plots and story lines that are relatable and easy to follow
-Topics children enjoy
-No more than 3 syllable words

Level 3 Waldorf Readers have larger paragraphs and words that will challenge and engage children/students.

Advanced Independent Reading   **Grade 2-4**
-In depth plot and story lines
-Larger blocks of text
-Full color illustration
-Words with 3+ syllables

Level 4 Waldorf Readers are more challenging and lengthy. These books are perfect for children/students who want to read longer books and still enjoy colorful illustrations. Level 4 Waldorf Readers are the last level before advancing to Waldorf Chapter Books.

Published by Waldorf Publishing
2140 Hall Johnson Road
#102-345
Grapevine, Texas 76051
www.WaldorfPublishing.com

Penny the Pineapple Visits the Great State of Virginia

ISBN: 978-1-63795-312-9

Library of Congress Control Number: 2021931572

Copyright © 2021

All rights reserved. No part of this book may be reproduced or transmitted in any form or by any means whatsoever without express written permission from the author, except in the case of brief quotations embodied in critical articles and reviews. Please refer all pertinent questions to the publisher. All rights reserved. No part of this book may be reproduced or transmitted in any form or by any means, electronic or mechanical, including photocopying, recording, or by an information storage and retrieval system except by a reviewer who may quote brief passages in a review to be printed in a magazine or newspaper without permission in writing from the publisher.

Illustrations by Ashley Kenny, Ellen Weisberg
Design by Baris Celik

Penny the Pineapple Visits the Great State of Virginia

Penny is a friendly and curious fruit on an exciting voyage to see the United States of America (U.S.A.), a beautiful land and the third largest country in the world.

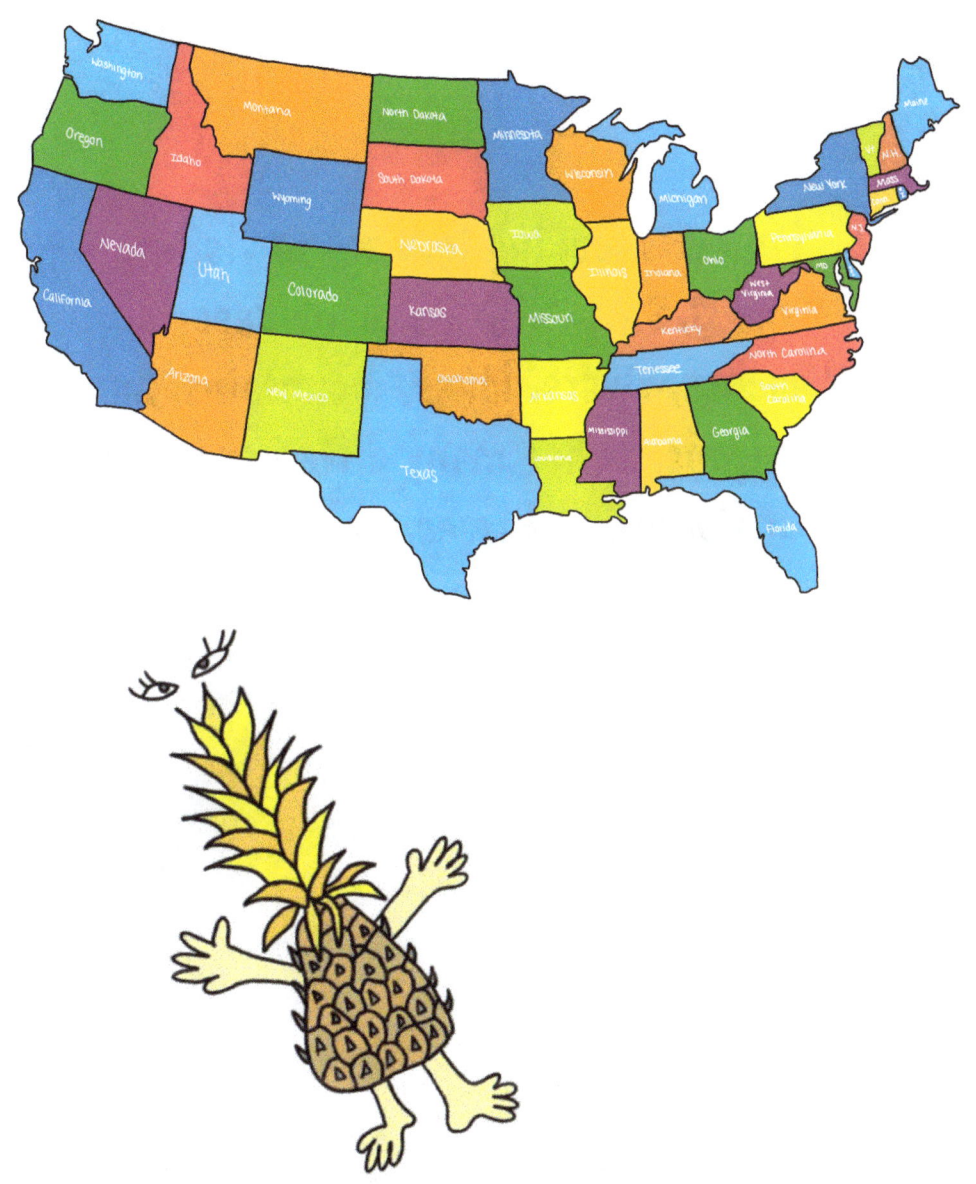

Penny is looking forward to visiting the U.S.A., with its many deserts, beaches, rivers, lakes, mountains, and canyons. It has many different kinds of flowers and trees, and birds and animals, and crops.

There are a whopping 300 million people living in the U.S.A., across a wide range of cultures!

The sweet, but sometimes sour, Penny has a tendency to misplace her crown. As she searches for her missing leaves, she will discover the great state of Virginia.

Penny encounters fun new places while exploring "The Old Dominion State." She visits her friend, Richmond, who is named after the state's capital.

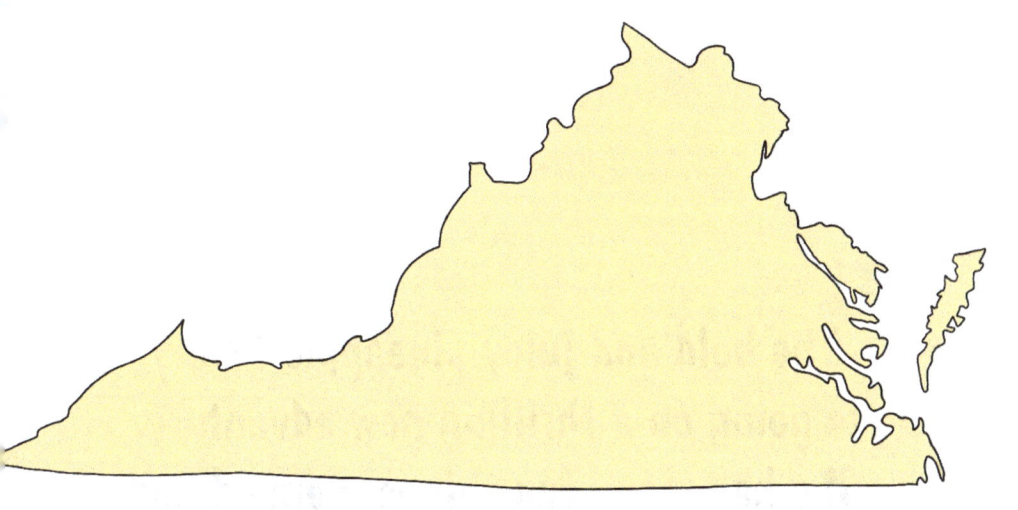

The bold and juicy pineapple Penny is going on a thrilling new adventure. She has many fun things planned and places to see and friends to visit.

She will travel down the east coast to the Mid-Atlantic region, where she will visit the states of Pennsylvania, Delaware, West Virginia and Virginia.

Lucky Penny has friends to see at every stop!

Today, Penny is visiting the great state of Virginia in the Mid-Atlantic region. Will you join her as she discovers new places?

"What state is this?" Penny asks as she heads for a city in the distance.

Wanting to look her very best for her visit, she reaches up to straighten her crown. But she finds that it is missing!

"Shoot!" Penny cries.

She cannot remember where she might have lost it. She wonders if perhaps it may have slipped off while she was hiking. "I don't want to be a drama queen, but I really need my crown."

Perhaps you can help her find it along the way?

Curious to see Virginia, Penny travels over the Allegheny and Blue Ridge Mountains. Here her pal Richmond ("Richie" for short) lives in the eastern part of the state, near Chesapeake Bay and the Atlantic Ocean.

Together, they visit the towns of Norfolk and Virginia Beach, take a swim, and admire the Flowering Dogwoods, the state tree and flower.

Penny is impressed by Virginia, with its scenery ranging from mountains to beaches, but she wonders why it is called "The Old Dominion State."

Richie explains that Virginia's nickname comes from the fact that it was England's first colony in the Americas.

"Have you seen my crown, Richie?" Penny asks. "I know it's a thorny topic, but I really need to find it!"

"I don't see it," Richie replies. "I'm so sorry!"

Richie tells Penny that Virginia's state bird, like West Virginia's, is the Cardinal. Of course, Penny also knows that the state tree is the Flowering Dogwood and the state flower is the Dogwood.

Penny also learns from her good friend that Virginia was the tenth state to join the U.S.A.

Number 10- admitted to USA - Virginia!

Penny happily tells Richie that she's thought of a poem during her visit. She asks him to give his opinion after she's finished reciting it:

Richmond lived for years on Virginia's coastal plain. The east shore was his home, his pride, and his domain. But the Blue Ridge mountains would beckon him away from Norfolk, Virginia Beach, and Chesapeake Bay.

"That is an excellent poem!" Richie happily yells. Richie can tell from the way the poem is written that Penny really understands Richie's great love for his state.

He thinks her poem reveals all of the most important points about the great state he calls home.

"I think I'm drained now," Penny decides. "But I'm really pining for my crown. I've seen all of Virginia and still cannot find it."

Just then a sack of soybeans suddenly tips over, and soybeans spill out and roll all over the floor. One soybean tumbles and lands on a part of the floor that is exactly where Penny's crown is lying.

"Well by golly, my crown! In the flesh." Penny picks it up and tucks it snuggly back on her head. "Time to put down my roots and rest," she yawns.

Will you meet Penny on her next adventure?

THE END

CPSIA information can be obtained
at www.ICGtesting.com
Printed in the USA
BVHW010203191021
619288BV00010B/302